Committed Cowboy

Whiskey Run, Cowboys Love Curves
Book #5

Kaci Rose

Five Little Roses Publishing

Copyright

♥

Roses Publishing have been granted permission to write in the Cowboys Love Curves spin off.

Book Cover By: Yoly @ **Cormar Covers**

Editing By: Debbe @ **On the Page, Author and PA Services**

Proofread By: Nikki @ **Southern Sweetheart Services**

Blurb

♥

He's her best friend. She's been his, since high school, only she doesn't know it. But she's about to find out with a little help from a small-town and a good friend.

I have a secret no one knows.

I'm in love with my best friend.

We dated in high school, and then she went away to school, and I took over my parents' ranch.

We stayed best friends, and to keep her, I may have done something stupid...like sabotaging all her dates and relationships kind of stupid.

This time I think I went too far.

When she shows up pissed and pounding down my door, I don't think either of us are ready for what happened next.

Do you love curvy women, possessive cowboys, friends to lovers, and second chances? What about a guy who knows what he wants, small-towns, and steamy romance? Then, you'll love Garrett and Kaylee's story.

Whiskey Run is home to the sexiest and most possessive cowboys you'll ever find. They work hard and play even harder. They might be gruff and bossy, but all it will take is the right curvy woman to bring them to their knees. Welcome to Whiskey Run...where the cowboys know how to ride.

Dedication

❤

To all the friends out there debating taking that next step.
  This is your sign.
  Jump.
  It will be worth it.

Contents

Chapter 1

❤

I hate blind dates. Becca, who I work with, set me up with one of her brother's friends. She has shown me his photo and swears he's seen mine.

This guy is good looking don't get me wrong, but as a curvy girl, I think I carry more anxiety than most over blind dates. It's one thing for a guy to see you in person and ask you out, but it's another for them to just show up without seeing me beforehand.

On the last blind date, I had the guy take one look at me, and then turned around and walked out. Curvy girls aren't for everyone, and I'm okay with that. In fact, I think it weeds out some of the assholes.

I love my body and don't have any plans to change for anyone. It just means dating is a bit harder for me than many of my friends.

"Girl, that dress looks hot!" Becca says.

She's on a video call with me, as I get ready. As much as I hate this blind date, I'm happy to have an excuse to wear this dress I picked up on sale last month. Though I didn't have any place to wear it, I had to have it. I learned a long time ago when I find something that's flattering on my body, to pick it up right then and there.

It's a blue floral print with a tight bodice, making my boobs look amazing and perky, and then, it's loose from the waist down, hugging my hips perfectly.

"He's going to swallow his tongue with you in that dress, girl. If I wasn't straight, I'd do you in that dress!"

"Becca!" We both burst into giggles.

She's one of those friends who tells it to you like it is and doesn't have a filter. So, I know when she says something, it's the truth. Though, it can backfire sometimes, like when it comes to setting me up on dates.

"Okay, now. Go put some curls in your hair, and you will be the hottest girl in the room tonight, no matter where he takes you."

"I doubt that but thank you. Just remember, if this date is a dud, you'll be buying me lunch at work for a month!"

"I promise. Now go!"

We hang up, and I head into the bathroom to put some curls in my long, dark brown hair. My hair has always held curls very well, so it's my favorite way to wear it. Even if most days, I just let it air dry because I don't want to put the energy into it.

I'm just finishing up with the curls when Garrett calls.

We have been best friends, since elementary school. We did everything together, and I do mean everything. We even lost our virginities together. When I went to school in Jasper, he stayed behind to work his parents' ranch and take online business classes.

Since then, he's taken over his parents' ranch, while I've gotten a job working in human resources for a family owned company in Jasper. We see each other a few times a month and talk several times a week.

Back home in Whiskey Run, he has a reputation as *The King of No Commitment*. The girls complain, but he's been nothing but nice to me, so I ignore the rumors.

"Hey," I answer the phone

"What are you doing?" He asks.

There's some slight noise in the background, and I know that sound well. He's in his truck driving somewhere and wants to kill some time.

"Getting ready for a blind date."

"No way. Not tonight. I'm in town."

"Why didn't you tell me you were coming to town? I'd have cleared my schedule."

"It was more of a last-minute thing and just for the day. Cancel your date and let me take you to dinner."

Even though I don't want to disappoint Becca, there's no way I'm passing up dinner with Garrett. I know I will have a good time, and he's pretty easy on the eyes. There's something about a cowboy in wranglers and boots that just does it for me.

Plus, I always get a kick out of watching the girls flirt or try to hit on him when we are together. He ignores them and won't flirt back. When I asked him about it once, he said it's out of respect for me. I told him if he wanted to pick up a girl he could, but he didn't like that idea at all. So now, I just enjoy the show.

"Okay, how long, before you get here?" I ask.

"Fifteen minutes."

"Good thing I'm ready to go out."

"See you soon." He says, and we hang up.

Glancing at the clock, I can see that the chances are Jason hasn't even left his house yet, so I shoot him off a quick text, saying some family came into town unannounced, and I'd like to reschedule.

Then, I take a deep breath to steady my nerves and call Becca.

"You are not changing that dress. You look killer in it."

"That's not it. Don't get mad, but I'm going to reschedule the date."

"Kaylee! What? No! Come on, you need to get out there. Plus, you look gorgeous, and I swear this guy is a good one. He likes curvy girls, and he's hot. Don't do this," she pleads.

"Garrett just called. He's in town, and we are going out to dinner," I tell her.

She laughs, but I can hear the sarcasm in it.

"Of course, he is. Didn't you tell him about this date on Monday?"

"I think I did, but he said it was a good idea, just like you did."

"Right. Well, let me know how dinner is, and I'm going to hold you to rescheduling with Jason."

"I promise," I say, just as there's a knock on my door. "He's here. I have to go."

We hang up, and I walk through my small apartment to the door, checking the peephole before opening, because he will be making sure I do.

When I open the door to the sight of Garrett, my heart starts to race, like it always does. Wranglers that hug him just right, and his strong muscular body brings a flush to my face. He's in his dressier boots, the kind he wears to town or to meetings, and not the ones he wears to work on the ranch. And his outfit wouldn't be complete without a nice shirt and a cowboy hat in his hand.

Looking at him, I can't help but think, yeah, tonight is going to be better than any blind date.

·♥·♥·♥·♥·♥·

Garrett

I take a deep breath, before knocking on Kaylee's door. When I see her, it's always the same. Yeah, it's the same feeling I got, when I kissed her for the first time, or when I saw her naked for the first time, and when I made the vow to her one night, that I still plan to uphold.

Every time I see her, it's like a field of butterflies are in my stomach, and the breath gets knocked out of me. Kaylee's the most beautiful girl I've ever seen, and even more so since she went to college and has developed those stunning curves. The curves I'd do anything to get my hands on.

So, as much as I try to prepare myself, it never quite works. When I knock on the door, and she answers in a blue dress that sets off her baby blue eyes and hugs every curve, I know I still don't have it together. I was prepared for her to be in jeans and a cute top, but not this sexy dress.

Thankfully, I have a moment to get myself together, as she checks me out, too. I just hope she doesn't notice I've taken my hat off and am holding it in front of me to hide how hard she makes me. That has been a challenge to hide from her for years.

"You were going to go on a date wearing that?" I ask her with a smirk.

"Yes. Why? What's wrong with it?" She looks down at the dress.

"You are asking for trouble, baby girl. That dress gives a man ideas you might not be ready for." I know I'm talking about myself, but she assumes I'm talking about her date, and I just go with that. No point in stirring up that hornet's nest.

"Well, Becca picked it out, and I love it, so it's what I'm wearing." Looking at me, she holds her head up a bit higher. She's always been a stubborn one, and it's one of her best qualities in my opinion.

"You ready to go?" I ask her.

She grabs her purse and locks the door behind her. "Yep, let's go."

I place my hand on the small of her back just for a bit of a connection. Then, I lead her to the elevator and down to my truck, where I open the door and help her in. Though she always assumes I do this to be a gentleman, but my motive behind it is so that I can touch and get my hands on her, even for a brief moment. Plus, the view of her ass is not only spectacular but a perk.

Taking her to our favorite BBQ restaurant downtown, we get a table and sit in the back. We spend the night talking and catching up. Even though we have been friends, since we were kids, now we have jobs, bills to pay, and adult responsibilities, and are only able to grab dinner together like this one or twice a month, if we're lucky.

I miss being with her. Though we talk every day on the phone and text, it's not the same as seeing her in person. It's just different. As we finish up, and the waitress brings the check, she tries to pay for her half. We go through this every time.

"Not a chance. I asked you to dinner, made you cancel your plans, and I'm paying." I tell her.

"But you came into the city, so I should pay," she pouts.

"I was here anyway, meeting with a supplier, and there was no way I was passing up a chance to hang out with you."

"Okay, but I'm buying ice cream," she says.

"Deal," I agree.

We always go for a walk after dinner and end up at the handmade ice cream place, where we get a cone and eat it while walking the rest of downtown.

I love our little routines and look forward to them.

Walking downtown tonight, with the air cooling off, and the lights on Main Street, shining in the dark, reminds me of the promise we made to each other a few years ago.

Every day we were watching her mom die a little more from cancer, and it was the worst time in both of our lives. Her parents were like a second mom and dad to me, so it was hard to see. Because her parents started a family late and were older, when the surprise pregnancy happened, she was their only child.

One night, Kaylee said she wanted to start a family young and have a few kids. I agreed with her, and at that moment, we made a promise. If neither of us were married by the time we were thirty-two, we'd marry each other and start a family within a year.

She made me promise and gave me a huge list of reasons why I should agree. What she didn't know was I didn't need all of those reasons, because I'd have agreed the moment it came out of her mouth, if she had let me. That night, Kaylee sealed her fate.

I have been in love with this girl for as long as I can remember. Her going off to college put space between us, but I think it was for the best. We were both still young, and I was taking over the family ranch, while she was getting her degree. At that time, I don't think it would have worked out.

But then, we made that vow her senior year, and she became mine that night, even if she doesn't know it. Though really, she has always been mine, but I promised myself that night I'd make sure of it. She had things she wanted and desired to do, and I needed to get our life set up for us.

As we eat our ice cream and walk, I fight the urge to take her hand in mine and to lick the ice cream off the corner of her mouth. She has made it clear that she has friend zoned me, and I'm good with that for now. Neither of us is ready to settle down just yet.

But she has always been mine and always will be.

Chapter 2

♥

Kaylee

I'm sitting at my desk working when Becca walks up and sits on the edge of my desk. "You do realize that Garrett is in love with you, right?"

"Don't be crazy, Becca. We're friends, and he loves me like a friend, just like I love him like a friend. That's all it is."

"You really don't see it?" She sighs.

I save what I'm working on and turn to face her. "See what?"

"He uses that playboy thing to keep you and everyone else away, while the time ticks down on that weird arrangement you two have. He drops everything to be there when you need him. I've seen how he looks at you, too."

Did she come to work drunk? I don't know where this is coming from. Maybe, she's more upset about me canceling the date last night than I realized.

"That's not true. He drops everything, because we are best friends, and it's what friends do."

"Not like that, but okay, let's test it. You're going home to see your dad this weekend, right?"

"Yes," I say.

It's just me and my dad now. I go home to visit him every other weekend, and on the weekends I don't go, he comes here and spends time with me. He even has his own room at my place, though it's supposed to be a guest room.

"So, let's reschedule your date. I know Jason won't mind meeting you in Whiskey Run. You can have dinner at that diner you love so much. Just make sure Garrett knows the details about your date, and then, let's see what happens."

"Fine." I agree just to prove her wrong. "But when this doesn't go the way you're planning, you'll drop it and leave it alone, right?"

"I will, but when Garrett proves me right, you need to admit to yourself you have feelings for him," she says.

"That's easy because my feelings don't go beyond friendship."

"Yeah. We'll cross that bridge when we get there." She smiles and goes on, "I will schedule the date and text you the details."

I roll my eyes and get back to work, so I can leave a bit early and pick up dinner on my way home for my dad and me.

·❤·❤·❤·❤·❤·

As I drive from Jasper to Whiskey Run, Becca's words keep rolling around in my head. What if she's right? I want to believe them, but I can't let my head go there, because if she isn't, I can't lose Garrett's friendship.

After my mom died, my dad never remarried. It was Garrett's mom that did all the girlie things with me, and my dad tagged along. Bra shopping, prom dress shopping, and everything in between, we did together. I know it's his mom who will be there on my wedding day, when I have babies, and all the big life events. I can't lose her, too.

My dad never remarried, but he's happy with his life the way it is, and it works for him. But for him to find someone new, they would have to fit into his life, because he's too set in his ways.

I pull into the Red's Diner parking lot and take a minute to gather my thoughts. Judging by the cars in the lot, there will be enough people in there to pull off Becca's plan.

Here goes nothing.

I walk in, and everyone glances my way. Most smile and wave, while others give me the once over, before going back to their meals.

At the counter is Geo, Garrett's ranch manager. I remember when he started to insist we call him Geo. His name is George, but he said that name made him feel old. He's been Geo ever since.

"Kaylee!" Violet greets me from behind the counter.

"Hey, Violet. My dad should have called in an order," I tell her.

"He did!" She turns to check on it, and I glance around.

I see Drew Colson, who owns Colson Ranch. He's sitting with a young woman, who I assume is his wife, Jordyn. Garrett told me about them. I can't help but wonder if they are another one of Violet's matches. In this town, she has a reputation for setting couples up.

"It will just be a few more minutes. Sit and tell me what's new with you?" Violet says, pouring me a glass of sweet tea.

Well, it's now or never.

"Nothing much. Though, I'll be back in here tomorrow night, because I actually have a date. I had to cancel earlier this week, but he agreed to meet me here for dinner." I tell her, before taking a drink.

"Good for you!" She says, though it's not hard to tell her enthusiasm is fake. "He lives there in Jasper, too?"

"Yeah. I don't know much about him. My friend, Becca, set me up with him."

"Well, I can't wait to meet him." She turns around to get something behind her.

A moment later, she's back with a bag in her hands.

"Here is your food. I threw in a few pieces of our Apple Cinnamon Blaze cake. I know it's both you and your dad's favorite." She says with a wink.

Smiling, I thank her, before heading out of the door. Geo is studying me and nods his head, before turning back to the gentleman next to him. Most of the people are trying to act like they aren't looking at me, but they are.

They heard my comment about the date, and it will be all over town, before bedtime tonight. It's certain Garrett will hear about it, and the only uncertainty is who will tell him.

If I had to put my money on it, I'd go as far as saying Violet is calling him up right now to update him, before I even make it to my dad's place. Violet is almost as bad as Becca is with matchmaking. Not only will she not leave anything to chance, but she has not hidden the fact that it's her opinion that Garrett and I should be together.

What would she think, if she knew our past, and what happened on prom night? I think she'd be pushing us together even faster.

·♥·♥·♥·♥·♥·

Garrett

I'm in the barn with the baby horse that was born last night and his momma. My dad tried to drill into me that we don't call it a baby horse, and it's called a foal, but I never broke the habit. To this day, I still call it a baby horse.

Even though I grew up on this ranch and have seen many births, it always amazes me how fast the horses stand after birth. My dad told me when I lose that amazement, it's time to retire. So, I hope I never do.

I'm leaning against the stall gate, staring at the baby horse feeding, when a truck pulls up. I don't pay much attention to my ranch managers. Geo went into town a while ago and is probably back.

He joins me in the barn a moment later.

"Kaylee's in town," he says.

"Yeah, she's visiting her father this weekend."

"Well, she's doing more than that. She has a date tomorrow night at the diner."

"What?"

A date? She just canceled the blind date the other night, and she already has another one?

"Yeah, that's what I heard her tell Violet," he nods.

I wonder why she didn't mention it to me. Then again, we haven't talked, since our dinner, and I've been wrapped up here with the birth.

So, I pull out my phone and snap a quick photo of the little horse, and then send it to her.

Me: This guy needs a name.

Kaylee: OMG! He's so cute!

Me: His momma struggled, and it's why I haven't talked to you in a few days.

Kaylee: Is she okay?

Me: Yeah, just tired.

Kaylee: Can I stop by, while I'm here, to see them both?

Me: You never need to ask. You're always welcome.

Kaylee: How about Sunday morning? I'll come early and make brunch. Tomorrow, I have plans with my dad.

Me: And a date, according to Geo.

Kaylee: Ah, the date I canceled, when I had dinner with you. We rescheduled, and he's coming out here.

I hate him already. How much can you kiss up by coming all the way out to Whiskey Run for just a date?

·♥·♥·♥·♥·♥·

I've been on edge all day. No amount of manual labor seems to help me get this energy out, and I hate feeling this way. I've resorted to moving the hay bales in the barn from one side to the other for no reason whatsoever.

"Okay, enough. Go get showered and head into town. We all know that's where this is going. Why you insist on keeping that girl at arm's length, I will never know," Geo says.

"I don't know what you're talking about," I say, wiping the sweat from my forehead. "And you know why." I level him with a glare.

He just shakes his head at me. "Get out of here."

I jog back up to the house and shower, shave, and get ready like it's me she's going on a date with, even though it's not.

It should be, but it's not.

Even though I should, I don't have a plan. So, I just drive to the diner and decide to simply have dinner at Red's Diner. I head straight to the counter where Violet is and smile at her.

"Hey there, Violet. How is JJ?" I ask about her son.

"Oh, he's doing well! Growing like a weed. Ledger and Liv are over there, so you make sure to congratulate them on their engagement before you leave. You here to eat dinner or cause trouble?" She winks at me like she knows why I'm really here.

When she nods to the corner over my shoulder, she confirms it. I turn to see Kaylee there with some skinny guy, who couldn't fill out a pair of wranglers if his life depended on it. What does she see in him?

There's a twinkle in Violet's eye like she knows exactly what I'm about to do. "I'll have my usual, Violet," I say and tap the counter in front of me, before standing up.

I stop at Ledger and Liv's table to congratulate them on their new engagement, but I never take my eye off of Kaylee. After no more than a few words, I go right over to where Kaylee is.

She's sitting along the wall where there's one long booth, a table, and then on the other side, a chair. Thankfully, she's on the booth end, so I just slide in right beside her and throw my arm over the back of the booth behind her.

"Hey there. Who is this?" I ask, nodding to the city boy across from me.

"Garrett, what are you doing here?" She asks, not sounding a bit surprised to see me.

"I came to get dinner. With the horse's birth and all, no one really has time to cook right now, and I needed a break. Geo got to come into town earlier, so it was my turn. Are you still coming by tomorrow to see the new addition? She doesn't have a name yet." I add, knowing that thinking up a name is her favorite thing to do.

"Yeah, I'll be by like I planned. Oh, and this is Jason. He's friends with Becca's brother, and we're making up for the date I canceled on earlier this week," she says.

Huh. A makeup date so soon? And he drove all the way out here for it? I eye him up, wondering what game he's playing.

"Jason, this is my best friend, Garrett. We grew up together. You can think of him as my overprotective older brother," she says and elbows me in my side.

I grunt and bring my arms down to protect myself in case she gets any ideas to do that again. Older brother? I think not.

"Come on, sweetheart. There's nothing brotherly about what we did after prom," I smirk and watch her eyes go big.

We don't talk about us sleeping together, but I can tell Jason here is already nervous with me being her friend. If he knows we slept together, there's a good chance he won't be comfortable with me in the picture at all, and she has dumped guys for less than that.

Watching Jason, I know I'm right. He's very uncomfortable now, shifting in his seating and checking his phone. If I'm right, he's going to make up some fake emergency and have to leave.

"Oh, hey. My mom texted, and she needs me to run and pick up her medication refill. I better go, before the pharmacy closes. It was great to meet you both, and Kaylee, I'll call you later."

He bolts out of the door before either of us has a chance to say anything. The moment he's gone, she turns and hits me in the chest.

"What the hell is wrong with you?" She says so loudly that the whole diner stops to look at us both.

"He isn't the one for you," I stand up and toss some money down on the table to cover her food. I head over to the counter, get my food from Violet, and then stomp out without looking back.

I don't have to look behind me, because I can feel the daggers she's shooting me from here.

Chapter 3

♥

All night I was up stewing over Garrett's actions last night. Part of me knew he'd be there at the diner, but I didn't know he'd act like that.

I called Becca, mostly mad that she was right. She was surprised and wanted to know why I was. I didn't have an answer for her, and that angered me even more.

Knowing I need to talk to him about this, and since I promised to go to his place today, I guess today's the day. Besides, I want to see the new horse, as I'm a sucker for baby animals.

He knows that, too.

Damn him.

I don't know how I'm going to bring this up, but if I know anything, it won't be the second I step foot on the ranch.

As I drive up to the house that has been like a second home to me, I realize how little it's changed from when we were growing up.

Garrett's kept everything the same from the horns his dad put over the front door to the front porch swing his parents put up for me to read on, when I was over, even if his mom used it more than I did.

It feels like coming home, and I want to enjoy it for at least part of the day.

When Garrett steps onto the front porch, I'm just stepping out of my car. He looks hesitant and knows he's in trouble. I'm sure he thinks I'm here to yell at him. Good.

He's even more shocked, as I walk into his arms and hug him tight.

"We'll talk later, but I need a day with my best friend first," I mumble. He nods and holds me even tighter.

"Whatever you want to do, I'm yours for the day," he says, as we pull away from each other.

"I want to see the new horse, and then go for a ride."

He nods, and I follow him out to the barn to the birthing stall.

The little horse, the color of warm caramel, is adorable, following his mom around the stall. But he's got the temper of a wild hornet, which is evident by his anger that his mom won't stand still for him to nurse.

"Is he always like this?" I ask.

"He's stubborn, pushy, and loves to cuddle, once he has a full stomach," Geo says, walking up and giving me a hug.

"Tattletale," I whisper in his ear, which earns a chuckle from him and a glare from Garrett.

"He's a firecracker," I smirk.

Garrett just shakes his head.

"That what you want to name him?" He asks.

"Yep."

"Alright, Firecracker it is."

He pats the stall gate and strides to the other side of the barn, where our horses are, and we silently prep for our ride.

It isn't until we are on the trail that leads to the creek that he breaks the silence.

"How mad are you?" He asks.

"Not as mad as when you put the spider in my hair, but angrier than when you pushed me fully clothed in the creek and killed my phone."

His Adam's apple bobs, as he swallows hard and nods, but looks right ahead.

The night he put the spider in my hair was the summer heading into ninth grade, and I physically tried to kill him. His dad had to hold me back. It's been our measuring point since then. I haven't been that mad since, but this is a very close second.

The ride reminds me of old times, and the longer we ride, the more we loosen up, and he starts smiling and joking. He tells me the story of Firecracker's birth, and then other stuff from around the ranch. After a picnic at the creek, we have fun brushing the horses down.

Once we walk inside the house, things get tense again.

"Any idea what you want for dinner?" He asks, going into the kitchen.

I shake my head. "Nah, I'll make dinner, as it's the least I can do," I say.

I hate to admit that I like how unsettled it makes him.

"I'll go get cleaned up," he says, hightailing it out of the room.

I get everything to make his mom's chicken casserole. Since I know it's one of his favorites, I'm hoping that maybe, I can butter him up to get the answers I need.

As I'm pouring us both a glass of whiskey, he steps into the kitchen again. Looking at him, he takes my breath away with how handsome he looks cleaned up.

He may be at home, relaxing in worn jeans and a t-shirt, but this isn't a side many people get to see. When he goes out in public, he dresses up to put his best foot forward, just like his mom and dad taught him.

I set the bottle of whiskey on the table with us, and we sit down to drink. While he doesn't say anything, he watches me warily.

Then, he takes that first bite of food, and his eyes close.

"It's perfect. I haven't had this, since they retired and move down to Florida," he says.

"I'm surprised they have stayed there this long."

"You and me both." He gives me a half smile.

As we finish our dinner and whiskey, I straighten my spine and take a deep breath.

"Why are you always sabotaging my dates and relationships?" I ask.

He stares at his plate and pushes the last bit of food around he was just raving about, but he doesn't answer me.

"I have a theory," I say.

"Yeah?" He asks slightly interested.

"Yep. I was up all night thinking about this. You want to make sure I marry you, like the pact we made. You use the playboy thing to push everyone away."

I study him, as I speak, and he starts shifting in his seat and acting really weird. Normally, I can tell how he's feeling, and what he's thinking just based on how he acts, but I can't read him, not this time.

"You've never lied to me before, so don't start now," I say with a pointed stare.

"Then don't make me answer that question." He says, almost begging me, as he stands up from the table.

Rising too, we both stand there and stare at each other. I may not have known how to read him earlier, but now, he's begging to stop this conversation. It's as if he can't admit his vulnerability, something I haven't seen in him for a long time.

I don't think I just act.

I lean over and kiss him.

Hesitating for only a moment, before he's kissing me back with urgency. His hands wrap in my hair, pulling me closer, and his body presses against mine, backing me up to the wall.

While I may have initiated the kiss, he takes control, cupping my head and tilting it exactly where he wants to deepen the kiss.

Just like all those years ago, this kiss stops time, and nothing else exists besides his mouth on me, his tongue tangling with mine, and the sparks he creates, shooting throughout my body.

Then, like he remembers who I'm supposed to be to him, he pulls back, acting like he's been burned, getting too close to the fire. Abruptly he crosses the room, running his hand through his hair like he does when he's lost in thought.

"I can't do this," he says, and then walks out of the room.

·❤·❤·❤·❤·❤·

Garrett

I don't even make it but one step into the living room. I should have known she wouldn't drop this. It isn't in her to let things go so easily.

"Why not?" She asks from behind me.

I can feel her right behind me. So close that, if I turned around, she'd be right there. So close, that I could kiss her, run my hands through her hair, and have my way with her. All the things I want to do, but I can't.

Forming two fists, I try to release the tension shooting through my body, before taking a few steps into the living room and turning to her. She's still standing in the doorway watching me.

"Because I'm horrible at relationships, and I can't lose you," I say with as much honesty as I can give her.

Not only has she been my best friend, since we were kids, but she was my first everything. I don't think I could handle losing her. I'd be so lost without her.

She crosses her arms, pushing her bountiful breasts up, and I curse myself for noticing. Then, she studies me carefully for a moment, like she can tell I'm not giving her the whole truth.

"Who says you are horrible at relationships?" She asks, raising an eyebrow at me.

I give a bitter laugh. It would be a shorter list to give her the people who haven't said it. Trying to find a way out of this conversation, I shake my head.

"I remember this between us being pretty damn good. So again, who says you are horrible at them?"

She's right. Things between us were good. But we were kids, barely eighteen, and now, so much has changed. We had a lot to learn back then and a lot of growing up to do.

"Every girl who has tried to tie me down," I admit.

She takes a step towards me, but I hold my ground. I should move away, but Kaylee has this draw to her that makes you want to be close to her, even when she's mad at you.

"Maybe, it's because they knew you had feelings for someone else."

Whoa! I jerk back. What the hell is she saying? How is she hitting so close to home? There's a reason I'm labeled a playboy. I knew what I wanted, and what I wanted was Kaylee, but there wasn't another version of her out there, so I didn't want to waste anyone's time.

Then, the small-town gossip mill started its work, seeing me with a different girl all the time. So, they gave me the playboy label, and I ran with it, happy to use it to keep a wall up.

I just shake my head. I'm not going to open that can of worms, especially not tonight.

"No, we can't."

How much did she have to drink tonight? Two glasses over dinner with me? Did she have any, while I was in the shower? She had to have had one or two because she isn't thinking straight.

"When you're sober tomorrow, you'll see that, too," I tell her.

She just stares me down, and I stare right back, not willing to budge on this. Not even an inch.

"Fine, but I'm staying here tonight."

Turning, she stomps off to her bedroom. My parents thought of her as their daughter, and once her mother died, she spent a lot of time here, while her dad worked and grieved. Even though she had been perfectly capable of taking care of herself, he didn't want her to be alone.

Only when I hear the slam of her bedroom door, do I collapse onto the couch.

What the fuck just happened?

Throwing my head back, I stare up at the ceiling. When she came over, I swear I thought she'd yell at me for ruining her date. Then, we'd talk about how she deserves to be treated like a queen, how a city boy won't understand her, and we'd be okay. She'd go home, and I'd give her a week to cool off. After that, we'd hang out next weekend, as if it never happened.

Instead, I'm sitting here at what feels like a crossroads at a bridge. I'm not ready to cross, but if I don't go across and just do nothing, I'll lose her forever. Instead, I feel like I'm being shoved over the bridge, and I don't like this feeling at all.

What the hell am I going to do?

I look around the living room. Everything is still in place from when my momma decorated it. The gray walls, natural wood furniture, and off-white sofas with hints of the deep reds you find around the ranch. Pulling the outside in, is what she called it.

This coffee table is the one Kaylee and I would sit at with my parents and play board games when it would rain.

To this day, I don't think we have made it through an entire game of Monopoly.

Someone always accused someone of cheating, and then the board would get thrown, effectively ending the game. How we still have all the game pieces I will never know.

This couch is the one we would snuggle up on and watch movies together. How many times did we fall asleep in each other's arms? I always cherished those nights, when I'd wake up with her in my arms and get to carry her to bed. I'd lay her in her bed and stand there to watch her sleep, before slipping into my room and dreaming of her.

Heck, how many times did she make dinner in that kitchen, just like she did tonight? She fits in here, and I can't think of even the slightest possibility of her not being here.

Finally, I pull myself up and get to work on cleaning up the kitchen and saving the leftovers.

I can't lose this girl. Yet, the thought of it being something more scares me too, because I know I'll mess things up. There's a reason I don't do relationships, but I feel like, if I don't give it a try, I'm going to lose her.

I'm stuck either way, but I know her. If I just give her time to cool off, she'll see I'm right. We are better this way, and it's not worth losing each other over. In the morning, I'll make her see it.

I don't have a choice.

Chapter 4

♥

Kaylee

After tossing and turning all night, I'm sitting in my bed at Garrett's house thinking. I thought over what Garrett said and also Becca's words to me.

Even though I considered calling Becca, I'm pretty sure her advice would be something along the lines of just grab him by the balls and kiss him. But she had been out drinking with her brother last night, and her advice any time she drinks, is to grab him by the balls and kiss him. Which isn't always helpful.

Looking around the room, I'm flooded with memories. This room was always my sanctuary, and it's different than any room in the house. My room is narrow but long, and my bed sits right against a full wall of windows, so I get a great view of sunrise on the ranch.

I'm pretty sure it was set up to be a nursery or an office, not a bedroom, but I love having my bed against the windows, and the view is one of the best on the ranch.

If I was having a problem growing up, I could sit here and watch the first rays of sunlight touch the ranch, and it seemed to fix anything, because nothing seems quite so big, after watching the sunrise.

Not today, though.

As I think over Garrett's actions the last few years, I realize Becca is right. He's either sabotaged any relationship I had, or he would ruin any chance I had of building one. Why would he do such a thing, unless he has feelings for me?

But he seems clear after last night, that he has no intentions of acting on those feelings. So, why keep sabotaging things? He's holding back a big part of himself because he doesn't want to lose me. I understand that, but he's lying to himself, saying he isn't good at relationships.

He's the standard I compare all guys, too. The few that lasted longer than a few dates, wouldn't have made it much further, because they didn't match up to Garrett. Though, I won't admit that to him. Instead, I'll let him keep thinking he stopped it from going any further by stepping in the way he always does.

As the sun starts to peek above the trees, I realize I can't put this off much longer, so I get up and get ready to go have breakfast. We'll have a talk, and then, I'll go spend some time with my dad, before heading back to the city.

After fixing my hair the best I can and brushing my teeth with the toothbrush I find in the cabinet, I open my bedroom door to a quiet house. I expected some noise, as the day was getting started. So, I make my way to the kitchen, only to find Garrett standing in front of the kitchen sink, just staring out of the window, watching the sunrise, much like I was in my room.

While we could have breakfast and dance around the subject, I don't want that. Instead, I decide to grab a cinnamon roll, some coffee, and dive right in.

As I plate a cinnamon roll and start making my coffee, Garrett watches every move I make, but neither of us says a word. It's like if one of us talks, we break the spell of being able to pretend this is just another morning.

Once I'm finally sitting at the table, he joins me, and it's time to break the spell.

"Well, I'm sober and still feel the same way," I tell him.

He looks pained, which isn't what I expected, but he still doesn't say anything.

Then, he sets his coffee down and shakes his head.

"No." He says emphatically, as he stares across the table at me.

"So, what about our pact?" I ask.

"If the time comes, I will honor it. That doesn't change."

I stare him down, and he won't look at me. He just keeps looking through me to the wall behind me.

"You have undermined every relationship I've tried to have, so how am I supposed to find someone and be happy?"

"They aren't good enough for you."

But I don't believe for a minute that's the only reason.

"Who is? You?" I raise my voice.

I'm trying to stay calm, but I'm getting irritated and pissed off, just like I was last night. It won't accomplish anything if we end up yelling at each other.

But when Garrett cringes at my suggestion that it's him who is perfect for me, I know this isn't going anywhere.

"No, not me," he rasps.

Studying him, it's then I realize he seems to have gotten even less sleep than I have. In fact, I wonder if he got any sleep at all. His hair looks like he's been running his hands through it all night. The circles under his eyes are dark, and he's still in the same clothes that he wore to dinner.

I stand up, put my plate in the sink, and finish my coffee, before setting my cup in the sink as well.

"Fine. I'm going home, and I'm going to date the guy from the diner, unless you give me a good reason not, too."

I stand there and wait for him to say something. Give me an excuse that Jason's too city or he wouldn't understand our friendship, or that I wouldn't be happy with someone who has a corporate job. Any of the excuses he's used over the years, but he has nothing and says nothing.

His silence says it all. I just nod, turn around, and walk out of the door.

My mind is all over the place, and I don't remember driving back to my dad's until I'm walking through the front door.

He doesn't say a word about me not coming home last night, just asks me to join him for lunch, before I head back to the city.

I won't pass up lunch with my dad, but I just hope he doesn't plan to ask me questions I can't answer right now.

·♥·♥·♥·♥·♥·

Garrett

The downside of being a good boss is that your employees stick around forever. Like Geo. He's been on the ranch since I was a kid. When he was eighteen, he came here looking for a job. My dad took him in and showed him the ropes. He says he'll be buried on the ranch because it's his home.

I love that he loves this land as much as I do, but the problem is he has seen everything. He's watched me grow up and has watched me with Kaylee, and now, he's going to have a front row seat to watching me ruin it all.

In some ways, he's as bad as Violet, sticking his nose in things. I'm pretty sure he's teamed up with her to push Kaylee and me together, one way or another.

So, when we are moving cattle to the west field today, he doesn't hesitate to confront me.

"What did you do to piss off Kaylee this time? I saw her leave out of here early this morning, and I don't think I saw her so mad, since you put that spider in her hair," he says.

I glare at him with no intention of talking about this, but he has a way of getting me to talk, even when I don't want, too. So, before I know it, I'm telling him everything, starting with my trip to Jasper earlier in the week, and then having her cancel her date to have dinner with me.

Then, I tell him about her date at the diner and everything that happened yesterday, down to the talk this morning, before she left. I expect him to tell me I did the right thing, which is that she's better off without me, but that's not what comes out of his mouth.

"You're an idiot," Geo says.

"What?" I ask, completely shocked.

The last person to talk to be like that was my father. Heck, the only people to speak to me that way are my dad and Kaylee.

"Letting her go like that? You're an idiot."

He repeats it again in case I missed it the first time. Before I speak again, I stare at the cows in front of us to get my bearings. Geo is family, and I don't want to go off on him, even if my instinct is to tell him off.

"You don't know what you're talking about." I dismiss him.

"Listen, I've watched you both all these years. Even if you tried to hide it from everyone else, I know you two were together your senior year. You really think no one caught you the times you'd sneak into the barn? I just kept everyone away. Now, you just won't admit your feelings for that girl, but that doesn't change the fact that you have some strong ones for her."

He knew about us back then? Of course, he did. There isn't a thing that happens on this ranch that he doesn't know about, but he has no idea right now what he's talking about.

"I'm done talking about this." Is all I say, and we don't talk for the rest of the afternoon.

The second we're done moving the cattle, I shower and escape into town. I head to The Whiskey Whistler. It's a bar downtown with mostly locals frequenting it. While it's kind of run down on the outside, the inside is done up right. Something you'd never expect to see if you judge a book by its cover.

Heading straight to the bar, I order a whiskey and down it, but before the bartender can walk away, I order another.

The second one I sip slower, and I finally take a look around me. Like every night, there's a mix of single people and couples. Many of the couples are laughing and having a good time.

I want that. I want to be a couple, have someone to talk to, to dance with, and to share everything with. But I don't want just anyone. I want the kind of relationship my parents have. Not only were they each other's best friends, but they worked the ranch and problem solved together.

Early on, I decided I wasn't going to settle for anything less. My dad always told me he knew on the first date that my mom was the one. Maybe, that's how I got the playboy reputation by dating so many women. If I'm not feeling it by date two, I don't waste my time, while most don't even get a second date.

I don't sleep with them. Heck, I can count on one hand the girls I've slept with, and everyone that wasn't Kaylee felt wrong like I was cheating on her, even though I wasn't.

Somehow over time, it's become a game to the girls in town, trying to see who will finally get me to settle down. I stopped going on dates and put my head down to take care of the ranch and spend what time with Kaylee I could.

What I have always pictured is running this ranch with Kaylee. It was always her I pictured by my side. Even as kids, before I understood my feelings, I saw us working the ranch together.

But I've got to get out of my head, so I take a look around the bar. Chase and Josie catch my eye on the other side. They recently got their chance at happiness and watching the way Chase looks at Josie, well, it would make anyone want what they have.

Why couldn't it work out for me and Kaylee, too? It might not be easy as we'll have to work at it. I know that, but we have been through so much more than other couples will ever go through, and we are only stronger for it.

Watching how Josie looks up at Chase, with as much love in her eyes for him as he has for her, I know I want that. And I want it with Kaylee, and I plan to do whatever it takes to make it happen.

As I leave the bar, I know I can't lose her, and I want more than friendship.

It's time to get her back. Though I'll need a game plan, but I'll be going after her. Sooner rather than later.

Chapter 5

♥

Kaylee

As I'm finishing curling my hair, a knock on the door startles me. My date is early. Turning off the curling iron, I smooth my hands over my dress. It's okay that he's early, as I'm ready to go, anyway.

I grab my purse and open the door without checking the peephole, only to find Garrett on the other side. Freezing, I expect him to ask if I even checked to see who it was, but he doesn't say a word.

He's standing there staring at me with a heat in his eyes in a way that every girl dreams of having a man look at her. Those gorgeous hazel eyes are running over every inch of me in my black cocktail dress and heels, and he doesn't hide it.

"Did you go out with him yet?" He asks, when his eyes lock with mine.

I could play innocent and make him sweat it out, but I don't.

"I'm meeting him tonight," I say, letting my eyes roam over him in those well-fitting Wranglers, button-down shirt, which emphasizes his broad chest, and then down to his cowboy boots.

"No, you're not," he says, catching me off guard.

Then, he steamrolls his way into my apartment, closes the door behind us, and pushes me up against the wall beside the door. With him looking down at me, I can't think with him pressing his body into mine, pinning me to the wall.

My brain doesn't comprehend what's happening until his lips meet mine. It's like when the gun fires at the start of a race, and it's on to see who can dominate the race. Only this time, it's a kiss. He's angling my face towards his, but already, my hands are in his hair, pulling him even closer to me.

His hands roam down the side of my body and rest on my hips, teasing me with what's to come by pulling me closer to him. I can feel how hard he is, and how much he wants me. I want him just as badly, but as my hands start moving down his chest, he pulls back and rests his forehead on mine.

Neither of us move, as we catch our breath.

"Cancel your date." He orders, and we both stare at each other.

The look in his eyes is new. It's desperate and a little nervous. It's the same look he had when we took the leap our senior year and crossed the line from friends to something more.

Maybe, that's why I nod my head and don't question why.

"Okay," I whisper.

He lets me go and crosses the room still breathing heavily. I pull my phone from my purse, and then text Jason to cancel on him, yet again. This time I don't give a reason, because I don't have one.

Then, I set my phone down and stare back at Garrett, who is watching my every move. He walks towards me slowly and places his hands on my hips again.

"Change out of those fuck-me heels and put on your boots. Let me take you out on a real date."

Before I can answer, he leans down and kisses me again. This one is soft and sweet. Taking his time, he makes love to my mouth in a way that leaves me breathless.

When he pulls back, I whisper, "Okay." Because I can't think, as my mind is a blank.

Then, he moves back enough, allowing me to walk by to my room. I remove the heels, grab socks, and put on my boots. Looking in the mirror, I can see that the boots take the dress from dressy to casual.

After changing out my gold necklace for a turquoise one, and then grabbing a jean jacket, I hesitantly return to the living room, not sure what to expect.

As we leave my place, Garrett opens the door for me with a huge smile on his face. During the entire drive, neither one of us speaks. When we get just outside of town, the paved road ends, and we're on a dirt road.

After passing through a gate and parking beside an old wood barn, I finally ask.

"Where are we?"

He smiles that carefree smile I love on him so much.

"At a friend's ranch." He gets out of the truck and comes around to open my door.

Holding my hand, he leads me into the barn, and I gasp. There are twinkle lights strung overhead, making a beautiful canopy. The large barn doors, on the opposite wall, are open and overlooking a river, and in the center, is a table set for two.

He's a perfect gentleman, pulling out my chair and serving me the wine first. It's everything I've always imagined. Though, as we start to eat, I have to know.

"Why the change of heart?"

He hesitates only a moment, before answering.

"I hated the idea of you on a date with someone else."

I don't know what to say to that. Though I'm sure tonight as I think it over, I'll come up with a bunch of snappy comebacks, but right now, I just let it go.

The conversation comes easily, and the meal has all my favorites, proving how well he knows me. The date isn't anything over the top or extravagant, but it's us, and it's the best date I've ever been on, because I'm not worried about saying or doing the wrong thing.

Conversation flows, and we laugh and talk. It's not awkward, when he reaches across the table to hold my hand, or when he pauses the conversation just to look at me with a smile on his face. This is the first date that I don't want to end, and he seems to feel the same way.

"Come spend the weekend at the ranch with me. We can have your dad over for dinner, or whatever you want, but spend the weekend with me," he says.

This is the weekend dad would normally come to spend with me in the city. Since we don't have any plans, I know he won't mind a change, and he'd rather have dinner on Garrett's ranch any day than some fancy dinner in the city.

The only downside is there will be a lot of questions I know I won't have the answer to, not yet, anyway.

"Okay." I agree.

The smile that takes over his face is one that I haven't seen in a long time. It's blinding and radiates pure happiness. It makes my heart race.

I'm in so much trouble with this one.

Garrett

Tonight is the night Kaylee is coming to spend the weekend at the ranch. I have dinner going, because she texted, saying she's on her way. Though I kind of cheated a little, since it's one of my mom's lasagnas she put in the freezer for me, I'm serving salad and garlic bread, too. Earlier, I stopped by the diner and got Kaylee's favorite Apple Cinnamon Blaze cake for dessert.

Since our date night by the river, we're on the phone every night. We share every detail of our days and talk without any barriers. It's so much better than when we talked on the phone before. There were lines we didn't cross, but now, I can tell her how beautiful she is, and how much I miss her.

I'm finishing setting the table on the back porch when she arrives, and I meet her at the front door. She looks comfortable in her jeans, showing off those curves I love. But most of all, she's still hot as hell. Though she looks a bit nervous today, and I'm glad I'm not the only one.

"You made it." I smile at her and lean in to kiss her.

Intending for it to be a quick kiss, but her lips taste like cherries, and when she melts into me, I pull her closer. Then, I can't resist nibbling on her lips, but when she moans, I pull back, because if she keeps it up, I'll end up taking her right here on the front porch for the whole ranch to see.

"I thought we'd have dinner on the back porch. I know you like watching the sunset there." She helps me take the food out to the table, and I should have known when she calls me out on it.

"I've always loved your mom's lasagna." She winks at me, after her first bite.

"Busted. Mom did stock my freezer for me the last time she was here. It has saved me from running to the diner for dinner more times than I can count."

She shakes her head with a smile.

"I should show you how to use your slow cooker. You put the food into it in the morning and dinner is ready, when you're done for the day."

"I'd still find a way to screw it up." I shake my head ruefully.

"Of course, you would." She laughs, and we talk about my parents, and what they are up to.

That turns to talking about her dad, and what questions he'll have for us when he comes over for dinner tomorrow.

Once we've finished eating and have cleared off the table, we settle on the couch on the back porch to watch the sunset. I sit on one end, and she sits on the other, but turns sideways and rests her legs over my lap.

A million times we have often sat like this, watching the sunset. From here, the house is on a bit of a hill, so you can see down a large portion of the ranch fields.

Tonight though, it feels like so much more than simply watching the sunset. For once, I don't have to hide the fact that I want to watch her and not the sunset. When she catches me staring at her, she smiles.

It's that smile that draws me in. I lean over and kiss her like I have wanted to do so many times when we would be sitting here just like this. Cupping her face and feeling her pressed against me, is something I've only imagined.

Though, we miss the sunset, because we can't stop kissing each other and making out like teenagers.

"Let's go inside," I whisper between kisses, but we barely make it in the door, before we're doing some heavy petting.

My lips glide down her neck, while I run my hands under her shirt. When she starts to go for my belt, I stop her.

"I want *you*, and not just sex. We don't have to do this." I tell her, but I'm still unable to keep my lips off her skin. I feel like there's so much we should talk about before we take this step, but none of it comes to mind right now.

"I want this." She reaches down and pulls her sweater over her head.

"Christ," I say, as I stare at her in her black lace bra with her luscious breasts and sexy curves on display.

Guiding her to my room, I'm still kissing her and running my hands over every inch of her body. I only stop to turn on the light and pull my shirt off, before my lips are back on hers.

Then, I reach around and remove her bra, before taking a step back to look at her. She's the most beautiful woman

I've ever seen. As my eyes roam over her, she tenses up and starts to cover herself.

"Don't hide from me," I growl.

She stiffens and won't look at me.

Placing my fist under her chin, I turn her eyes back to me.

"What is it?" I ask.

"My body has changed a lot, since the last time you saw it."

Until she speaks again, I don't get her meaning.

"Maybe, we can turn the lights off?"

"Oh, hell no. You are not hiding from me."

How does this girl not know how much I love these curves? I take her hand and place it over my rock-hard cock.

"Your body is so damn sexy. You feel me now. I'm always hard around you. You've never seen it because I've just gotten good at hiding it. So, no, I'm not turning the lights off, because I want to see every gorgeous inch of you."

With that, I kneel down in front of her and slowly peel off her jeans and her black lace underwear that matches her bra. Then when I stand, her hands are on me, removing my belt and jeans, until we are naked in front of each other.

While this isn't the first time we have had sex, it feels like the first time all over again. But now, it's more intense and life changing, because there's no backing out after this.

"Lay down on the bed, baby girl." I reach into my nightstand for a condom and put it on, all the while, knowing I won't last long.

I crawl between her legs and run my hands up the inside of her thighs until I reach her core. Running a finger through her slit, I find her soaked. As I play with her clit, she moans with her eyes closed.

Wanting more of her, I lean down, spread her thighs, and get my first taste of her.

"Garrett." She groans. "You don't have, too." She tries to pull me up to her.

"I know I don't have to, but I want, too. You have no idea how long I have wanted to taste you. How much I hated the fact that I didn't get a chance to do this before."

We were young, and I didn't know much back then. I never got the chance to go down on her, but I'm not making that mistake this time. Getting lost in her taste, I run my tongue over her again.

Taking my time, I slowly drive her crazy. Though, I could stay down here all day and have her come over and over again, until she passes out, and then only to start all over again when she wakes up. But the only thing stopping me is that I want even more to be inside her. Just as she gets close to falling over the cliff, I pull away, and she lets out a frustrated groan.

"After all these years, you are going to come for the first time on my cock." I tell her, and I kiss up her belly, between her breasts, and to her neck, before settling between her thighs.

She spreads her legs and wraps them around my waist like she's afraid I'm going to change my mind. Not a chance.

Then, I lock eyes with her, as I line my cock up at her entrance. Our eyes stay on each other, as I slowly slide into her, and I swear it feels better than the first time. With a few thrusts, I'm fully seated in her, and she's digging her nails into my shoulders.

"You okay, baby girl?" She just nods.

Slowly, I start thrusting in and out of her, enjoying the feel of her pussy enveloping me. It doesn't take long before I'm ready to come, and I'm not sure I can hold back. When I shift my hips to hit her clit, the added friction is all she needs, as she screams my name, and her pussy starts gripping my cock so hard, that my vision goes black.

I have never come so hard in my life. Nothing has ever felt so right, as when I look down at my girl flushed from an orgasm I gave her. I'm still inside her, and the smile on her face tells me everything I need to know.

Then, I lean down and kiss her, before thrusting my hips into her.

"Again," I growl, and she giggles.

It's the most perfect sound in the world.

Chapter 6

♥

Kaylee

When I wake up next to a warm body, I freeze and forget where I am. That is until I open my eyes and see I'm in Garrett's room. Next to me in bed, is my best friend, who is also naked and passed out from the multiple rounds of sex we had last night.

Fantastic, amazing, life altering sex. I try to stretch a bit, and his arm that's over my waist just pulls me in tighter, not wanting to let me go. So, I lay there, enjoying his hold and taking a look around his room.

His room is mostly gray. Gray walls, gray chairs, gray carpets. The bedsheets are almost white, but still a soft shade of gray. As a joke our senior year, I bought him some red pillows to give his room some color.

The problem was when placed in his room of gray, the pillows looked almost a shade of dark pink. I remember laughing so hard at it, but those pillows are still here, sitting on his chair and giving some color to the room.

I smile, thinking about how all this time, he has had a bit of me in his room. When he shifts beside me, I look over at him with the smile still on my face.

With his eyes still looking sleepy, he whispers, "I like you waking up with a smile on your face."

"I can't believe you still have those pillows. When I gave them to you as a joke, it was even funnier, when they looked pink in here."

"Well, I kept them as a joke, just to rile you up. But then after you went off to school, I kept them, because they were a piece of you."

I lean in and kiss him, which quickly turns into more, and after three orgasms, I roll out of bed, claiming the need to eat. Getting dressed, I head to the kitchen to start some omelets.

As Garrett walks into the kitchen, he says jokingly, "I think we need to call this brunch and not breakfast."

He's right, as it's almost eleven a.m.

"When was the last time you slept in so late?" I joke with him, because I know he's been up early to do the morning chores every day, since he took over the ranch, and even before that.

"I don't know. Maybe, when I was homesick from school, and my mom insisted I rest?" He says, making the coffee for us.

When we sit down, he pulls me into his lap and keeps one arm around me, as we eat.

"You should come out to the barn with me, before going to see your dad."

I agree, nodding my head, and then we finish our breakfast, talking about anything and everything.

As I follow him out to the barn, I see the ranch with fresh eyes. Eyes of someone who might possibly consider living here. While this ranch has always been a home to me, I never thought about it as a permanent home. It was a place to stay for the weekend.

Now, I can't help but think, if things continue the way they are with Garrett, this place might be more than that, and the idea doesn't scare me.

Going to the barn to check on Firecracker, we also end up helping out with some of the chores in there. I'm surprised Geo isn't here to give us a hard time about getting such a late start, but that's good because it allows me to stay in my head about how life would be like here.

Every morning, I'd be up with the sun making breakfast, and then coming out here to help in the barn. Working side-by-side with Garrett is something I could get used to.

"Hey, you better go see your dad, so you two can be back in time for dinner," Garrett says, wrapping his arms around my waist from behind.

"Ahhh, yes. I will go field all the questions of what's going on with you, and then you can charm him with your cooking."

"With my mom's cooking, but yes." He kisses down my neck. "Now go, before I drag you back to the bedroom."

"Don't tempt me with a good time."

I smile over my shoulder, as I walk to my car. Even as I drive down the driveway and towards my dad's place, his eyes stay on me.

Pulling into the driveway, I don't waste any time sitting in my car, because my dad will already know I'm here. He has a good ear for people approaching his house. Plus, he's expecting me.

I walk in the front door and slip off my boots.

"Dad?" I call out.

"Study!" He calls back.

His study is one of the guest rooms he converted into a home office, and then put up a few bookcases to store his collection of books in. It sits right next to my room that I still use, when I come to visit and stay the weekend.

When I step into the study, Dad is just closing his laptop.

"Don't stop on my account," I joke.

"Oh, it was nothing important. Just reading some of the local news."

When my dad says local, I know he doesn't mean Whiskey Run. He'll read news about anything from here to Nashville, and even as far as Atlanta. But he still calls it the local news.

"So, tell me, daughter of mine, is this conversation one I need to pour wine or whiskey for?"

This is always how my dad would gauge how serious a conversation he and my mom were going to have. Once I turned twenty-one, he started doing it to me. Wine meant it was a normal conversation. Whiskey meant it was a hard topic or bad news.

"Wine for me, but I'm not sure for you."

This causes my dad to pause and look at me, and then pour himself some whiskey and join me in the living room.

"Okay, out with it. I'm assuming it has something to do with Garrett since we are going over there for dinner tonight."

I decide it's best to just rip off the Band-Aid.

"Garrett and I are... dating," I say, for a lack of a better word.

My dad stares at me but doesn't say a word, as he takes a sip of his whiskey. Finally, a smile crosses his face.

"Well, it's about time. Anyone with eyes can see you two are perfect for each other."

"Seriously?"

"Yes, the whole town knew you two would eventually end up together when you both turned around and really saw each other."

Dad stands and pulls me into a hug, as I stand there shocked. I had a feeling people like Violet would play matchmaker, but I didn't think the whole town saw it, much less, my dad.

Well, things just got a lot more interesting.

·♥·♥·♥·♥·♥·

Garrett

It's been a week since I've been able to hold my girl. Last weekend was perfect, having her in my bed and in my arms every night and waking up with her there.

Dinner with her dad went better than expected. Though, he did give me the dad talk about how to treat his daughter right, and how I have so much land, that no one would find me if I hurt her. But after that, it was just like old times, easy going and fun.

Kaylee and I talked all week. In the morning, as she got ready for work, we talked. Then, we texted all day, and then after dinner, we talked all night. How can two people, who have known each other their whole lives, have so much to talk about? But even when we don't, and just sit in silence together, it's perfect.

Going this last week without being able to touch her, is driving me mad. My bed is empty, and the house doesn't feel like a home without her there. That's why I moved things around and surprised her last night, coming into Jasper for the weekend.

When I suggested going to surprise her, Geo practically pushed me out of the door. He said I've been a big bear, since she left Sunday night, and insisted there was nothing important to do at the ranch.

To have her in my arms again was what I needed. I felt like I could breathe again. Today, I'm hanging out at her place, while she works. Though originally, she was working a half workday, but since she went in late, because I couldn't seem to let her out of bed, that means she's working, until dinner.

I plan to take her to the new place that opened up last month that she hasn't tried yet. If the reviews are to be believed, they are supposed to have these amazing burgers. We both love a good burger, so I'm looking forward to it.

My phone goes off, and after a quick check, I see it's her.

Kaylee: Just leaving work. See you soon!

A simple text has me smiling like crazy. What if it was like this every day? What if she was coming home to me every night? This is the dream I have, but things are still so new, that I might scare her off if I say them out loud.

I get ready for dinner, nothing fancy just my usual attire, and then head to the living room to wait for her. She doesn't live too far from work, so I know she'll be home any minute.

I'm scrolling my emails, making sure there isn't anything that can't wait when there's a knock on the door.

Who the heck could it be? Her dad knows she's spending the weekend with me. It can't be him, because he made us promise to stop by for lunch this weekend. Her friend, Becca, she just saw at work. A neighbor maybe?

Opening the door, I find the guy she was on a date with at the diner. What the hell is he doing here?

"What do you want?" I ask in a not so nice tone. One my momma would scold me over, but she isn't here, so I don't bother correcting it.

"I wanted to check on Kaylee. She's been dodging me and acting really weird. So, I wanted to make sure she was okay."

Just as he says this, Kaylee walks up. I know she heard him, because she looks from him to me, and then back at him, before plastering on her fake smile.

"Hey, Jason." She greets him.

"Kaylee. I just wanted to check on you."

"That's so sweet of you. I'm sorry about everything, but I've been really busy with work and all. And honestly, I just didn't feel it on our date."

Jason gives a dry chuckle.

"I understand that. I hope we can stay friends, for Becca's sake, but I don't want things to be weird," he says.

"Zero weirdness, I promise," Kaylee says.

He kisses her cheek and then leaves, and I stand there in shock, pissed beyond belief.

When she looks at me, she knows I'm pissed, too.

"What is wrong with you?" She asks, pushing her way inside her apartment.

I follow her in and close the door behind us.

"You didn't tell him I was your boyfriend? You gave him some bullshit excuse."

I stood there, waiting to be introduced and nothing. It's like I didn't mean anything to her, and what we had was a fling.

"Is that what you are? Because we never talked about it, and having that discussion in front of Jason, seemed inappropriate." She says, slipping off her heels and putting her bag away.

"So, what the hell am I to you? Just sex?"

Turning, I run my hand through my hair, and when she doesn't answer me, I have my answer. This isn't anything more to her. Of course, it's not. You can't have a relationship with a playboy, right? I grab my bag and walk out of there, not even bothering to listen to her calling my name behind me.

I get in my truck and head home. Stupid me for thinking she wanted me for anything more than to scratch an itch. To say she had the bad boy before she settled down with a guy like Jason.

Of all the people she could have used as a bad boy, why me? Why ruin our friendship? Having no answers, I drive straight to The Whiskey Whistler and ignore everyone, as I go straight for the bar.

My phone has gone off several times and looking at it, I can see several missed calls from Kaylee and several texts. Not answering them, I turn my phone off and order another whiskey.

I knew giving in and trying for something more was a bad idea. My idea of something more was the whole package. A girlfriend, a relationship, and eventually, a life together. Apparently, hers was only some sex, until something better came along.

I'm such an idiot.

Chapter 7

♥

After Garrett left, I called Becca in tears, not sure I could even explain why. I ended up at her house last night and on her couch just a mess. Sitting there with me, she didn't ask questions, but put on a sappy movie and handed me some ice cream.

I think that's why Becca and I are friends. When I don't want to talk about something, she doesn't push me. Yet, she knows when I need to be pushed, like going on that date with Jason.

This morning she made me breakfast, shoved me into the shower, and let me be, until now. I figured at some point today she would force me to talk, so I've been thinking of what I'm going to say to her.

"Okay, girl. It's after three p. m., and I'm pouring some wine, and then you are going to tell me what happened right now," she says.

Though I think I can talk, there's going to be some tears, I'm sure.

We head out to her back porch and sit on her porch swing. It's my favorite place in her house. The back porch is screened in, and she has a bunch of pillows on the swing, so it's really comfortable.

Many times, when we hang out, we end up here, drinking wine, talking, or just sitting and reading books. Like last month, when we both were reading this book, the girls at work were raving about it. We were determined to read it over the weekend, so we could join the conversation. So worth it.

When you sit out here, the view is so peaceful. The empty lot behind her is all overgrown trees, as well as the lot beside her, making it feel like you're all alone back here amidst the forest. It's the perfect little escape without really leaving the city.

She joins me on the swing, hands me a glass of wine, and looks me over. It's the look that says she isn't going to push, but it's time to talk. So, I spill everything from the last few weeks.

How he crashed my date with Jason to me confronting him at the ranch and our talk. How he showed up and made me cancel the second date with Jason, us dating, the weekend at his place, and dinner with my dad.

I tell her how we talked all week, and he showed up to surprise me, and how he waited for me, while I was at work yesterday. Then, I tell her about what happened, when Jason showed up, and how Garrett left. Then, how I ended up here.

She knew some of the details, but I filled in everything else. As I tell her everything, she listens and keeps both our wine glasses full. When I'm done, before she can even speak, I ask the question that's at the front of my mind.

"How would it even work? I'm here in Jasper, and he's back home. My job is here, and his ranch is there."

As if she can read my mind, her words are what I've heard my mom say many times. When I was starting to have feelings for Garrett, it was the advice she gave me right before she died. Maybe, it stuck in my head, because she gave some of her friends that same advice, while I was growing up.

"If you want it to work, you'll make it work," Becca says. "There are plenty of ways to do so, and you know it." She gives me the straight up no bullshit answer.

I do a double take, because I swear, I hear my mom's voice and not Becca's, as she says it. To fortify myself, I finish up the wine in my glass and fill it back up again.

"What if he doesn't want me back? I haven't heard from him, since he left, and I've called and texted. Normally, he would have at least texted me by now, because he never liked me worrying, if he was okay or not. I thought about texting Geo to make sure he made it home all right, but I feel like now that we are more than friends, that would be crossing a line."

"That boy is head over boots for you. Everyone can see it. He'll take you back, but you have to talk to him and mean it. Show him you want him and have a plan to make it work."

"It's the how I plan to make it work I'm a little fuzzy on. I want it to work, and there's no doubt about that. I just don't see driving back and forth the rest of our lives a solution."

Becca sighs and giggles. "Life would be so much simpler if you had just stuck with Jason like I told you. You're both here, and he was even willing to go to Whiskey Run for you."

"By simple you mean boring." I giggle, and just like that, the tension is gone, and we are laughing and joking around. Then, we talk about the disaster of a date with Jason. Even before Garrett showed up, it was a dud, even if I wouldn't give him the satisfaction of admitting that to him.

I put all things Garrett out of my mind, all things boys, and focus on Becca. She talks about this new guy in her department, who has all the girls drooling over him. There's a pool going around to see who he asks out first. So far, he's been polite but turned everyone down.

We give each other makeovers and watch the classic romances, *Pretty Woman* and *Dirty Dancing*. We crank up the radio and sing badly to the music, while dancing around.

It's everything you think a sleepover with your best friend would be in middle school or high school; not in your twenties, yet it's exactly what I needed.

That night, as I lay in Becca's bed in a sugar coma, a plan starts to form. A sense of peace comes over me, and I know everything will be okay.

Tomorrow, I will get him back.

Garrett

I didn't hear a word from Kaylee yesterday. Not a phone call or a text. I thought about picking up the phone and calling her to make sure she was okay, but I wasn't ready to talk to her.

Before we started dating, she would have been blowing up my phone, demanding to know that I at least made it home all right, and when I didn't answer, she would start blowing up Geo's phone and even going as far as asking her dad to drop by to check on me. So, when there hasn't been a word from her, I know I really messed up.

Not knowing what she's doing, or how she's doing is driving me crazy. I didn't even get a text before bed. Though, I probably should have texted her, because now it feels too late to do so. I miss talking to her, but more so, I miss being with her.

Unfortunately, I'm on edge and no closer to an idea to fix this than I was yesterday. Trying to work out my frustrations yesterday, I did all the manual labor, and I'm pretty sure I scared off the ranch hands.

"Geo, I'm going for a drive. I'll be back in a while." I tell him, after moving some hay around for no reason.

"Good idea, boss. Clear your head." He says, but I'm sure he will be happy to have me out of the way for a bit.

Heading to one of the ranch trucks, I drive down the dirt road that leads to the back of the ranch and end up by the highway. It has the best views on the ranch, and I won't have to be paying too much attention, since it will be empty.

Ever since I started driving, this is how I would clear my head. A nice, long, slow drive along the ranch through some of the pastures is peaceful and helps me think. I would roll the windows down, take in the fresh air, and sometimes, crank up the music. By the time I would make it back to the main house, my head was clear, and I'd have a plan of action.

My dad did the same thing, and I know Geo does it every now and then as well. I remember once my mom got so frustrated with my dad, that she told him to go for a drive. He was gone for hours, but when he came home, they talked, and they couldn't keep their hands off each other. I was about thirteen, and it completely grossed me out.

As I drive, I can picture Kaylee's face. I know I messed things up. All I saw was this other guy, who thought he had some kind of claim on her, and I saw red. She was right. We hadn't talked about what we are to each other, and with my reputation, I can't blame her for not wanting to assume.

I spent so much time pushing her away, that she was probably scared to push me too hard, thinking I'd up and run just like I did. All I wanted was to hear her tell this guy I was her boyfriend, and that she was mine. When she didn't, I was hurt and pissed.

Then, instead of talking to her the first time things got hard, I left and couldn't even pick up the phone to let her know I was okay. No wonder she stopped calling me. I was an asshole. Christ, I wouldn't want to talk to me either.

When we got together, I should have made it clear to her that she's it for me. I knew it years ago, and it's why I didn't even think twice about making the promise to marry her if we weren't married by thirty-years-old. I always saw a life with her and only her. If it wasn't her, it wouldn't be anyone else.

Whenever I thought of my wife, it was her I saw walking down the aisle to me, her being the mother of my kids, and running the ranch with me. She's who I want to come home to every night and wake up with every morning.

She was right. My other relationships didn't work out, because it was always her I saw in my future, and not them. I just didn't see us dating, and then figured by the time she came to me to collect on the pact we made, I'd be ready, and we'd get married and just slip into married life. I didn't give it much thought.

I should have stayed the other night and talked to her. My dad never walked out on my mom like that. He might have gone to the barn to cool off, but they always worked it out, before going to bed that night. I don't think they ever went to bed angry.

Am I too late to talk to her now? I could show up on her doorstep with flowers or chocolate and beg for her to talk to me, or even just to listen. I know I have to do something if I don't want to lose her. Even if she doesn't want to keep dating, I can't lose her, as my best friend.

I need to make a big gesture to show her I'm an idiot, and how sorry I am. It needs to be something that proves I know her; not some generic gesture anyone could do.

As I round the sharp corner into the trees, I come face-to-face with a cow in the middle of the road. I jerk the wheel to the side to avoid hitting the cow, but the truck skids.

I try to pump the brakes and slow the truck down. Though I didn't think I was driving that fast, but I also wasn't paying attention.

The truck spins, and I can't stop it. I hit something. A tree? The cow? I don't know, because the force of the impact jerks me around before everything goes black.

Chapter 8

♥

Kaylee

As I pull into the ranch, I debate driving around town and going over what I plan to say to Garrett one more time. But when Geo sees me and waves at me, I know that option isn't possible.

I take a deep breath and plaster on a false smile, as I park my car and get out to go talk to him.

"Hey, Geo!" I call in a fake, cheery sound.

He gives me a pointed look, and I know then he knows everything. I should have guessed. This is Geo who has known us both since we were kids.

"You better be here to fix this. He's all out of sorts, and his head isn't on straight," Geo says.

"That's the plan. Though, if I'm honest, I'm not completely sure how to fix it, because I'm not sure why he's mad. I feel like he picked something small to focus on and blame, but it's really something else."

"See, you know him better than anyone. When he told me what happened, I felt the same way. If anyone can get it out of him, it's you." Geo hugs me.

"Where is he?" I ask him.

"He went for a drive. My guess is he's sitting by the creek thinking." Geo nods towards the dirt road that runs through the ranch. I don't think my car will make it, as it's a small four-door and not really made for ranch life.

"Take my truck. It has a radio if you need me in case he's being stubborn. I'll be happy to give him a stern talking, too," Geo laughs.

"I might have to take you up on that." I take the keys from him and get in.

The local country music station is on, and one of my favorite songs is playing. I take a moment and just listen, before heading down the dirt road.

I know the area Geo is talking about well. Many times, I've found Garrett there lost in thought. Often, I'd end up there myself. It's a peaceful part of the ranch that looks out over the back of the ranch, and the water sounds are so relaxing.

We had our first make out session there. Hell, even our first kiss there. It just happened. We had been talking, and we just looked over at each other, and it was like two magnets pulled us together. I smile to myself. Of course, he'd go to think of me in a spot that held so many of our firsts.

Maybe, I'll lead with my favorite memory about the creek. Remind him of the good times, before we grew up and things got so complicated. Then, I will open up about my feelings for him. Be completely honest that I love him.

Smiling, I think about how it took Becca and a lot of wine yesterday to make me realize I love him. I guess I have all this time and was scared to admit it and risk losing him for good. Becca agrees that it's why guys never made it past date three.

I decided it needs to be out there. Put the ball in his court, so at least I know I tried, and did everything I could. That way, if it doesn't work out, I won't have any regrets. I won't be left wondering what if I had said this or done that.

As I round a sharp corner into the trees, I know I'm close, as the creek is just on the other side. My happiness at seeing him soon fades, when I see his truck smashed into a tree off the road and smoke coming from the engine.

I slam the truck into park and run, yelling his name. I'm terrified of what I might see, but I need to make sure he's okay at the same time.

When I reach him, he's slumped against the steering wheel facing the window with blood on his face and his eyes closed.

"Garrett!" I yell again and take a deep breath. Then, I go through the checklist my dad taught me to do if I came upon an accident. Check to see if they're breathing, and then look for a pulse.

His pulse is strong, and he's breathing. Then, I check and verify he's the only one in the truck. Don't move him, unless it's necessary. Call for help. Pulling out my phone, I see there's no reception this far back on the ranch. I don't want to leave him to go get help, but I don't have a choice.

Just as I get back in Geo's truck, I remember the radio. I pick it up and pray he's in the barn.

"Geo! Geo, are you there?"

It seems like forever, before he answers back.

"Kaylee, what's wrong?"

"Garrett crashed his truck. He's unconscious, and there's a lot of blood. The accident was at the sharp curve just before the tree line."

"Okay, I'll call for help and meet you there. Stay with him," he orders.

"Will do." I get out of the truck and head back to Garrett. Nothing has changed, and as I stand there, I take better stock of him. There's lots of shattered glass, and the blood seems to be coming from a cut on his forehead. While I'm trying to get a look at the rest of his body without moving him, Geo arrives in another ranch truck.

From that moment on, everything is hazy. Geo takes control, gets the emergency crew out, and they remove Garrett from the truck and then take him to the hospital. We follow behind the ambulance. Geo drives me, as I'm shaky. When we get to the hospital, they whisk him away behind the emergency room doors.

Geo and I are forced to wait and told to fill out forms. How do they expect you to concentrate on forms when you don't know if your loved one is alive or dead behind those doors?

Before I know it, my dad is there. Probably, because Geo called him. The moment his arms wrap around me, I start crying. I don't have to be strong anymore, because my dad is there to be strong for me. Geo tells him the details of what happened, and then we sit and wait.

When the doctor finally comes out, I'm terrified.

"Family of Garrett Hayes?" The doctor asks.

"That's us." The three of us stand and don't even flinch.

"He's still unconscious. As you know, he hit his head in the crash, so we're monitoring him. He has a few bruised ribs and lots of cuts and scrapes. For a few of them, he needed stitches. We had to give him a blood transfusion because he had lost so much thanks to the deeper cut on his leg. Now, it's just a wait and see for when he wakes up. Meanwhile, we'll be monitoring his brain to make sure he's okay."

"Can we see him?" I ask.

"We are getting him settled in his room, and then I'll have a nurse take you up. Keep the lights dim in there, because when he does wake up, harsh lights will be painful to him."

So now, we wait.

·♥·♥·♥·♥·♥·

Kaylee

From the moment they brought us back to Garrett's room, I haven't left his side. The doctor wasn't joking around about him being all banged up. He has cuts and bruises everywhere. His head is wrapped up because one of the biggest cuts was on his forehead, and that's where all the blood I saw came from.

He's connected to an IV and all sorts of machines. I try not to think too hard about what they do, because it can get a bit scary. Instead, I just sit next to his bed and hold his hand.

My dad has stayed with me. He goes and gets food, and then makes sure I eat. He called Becca and told her what was going on, so she could tell work. She's covering for me there, and even packed me a bag of clothes with my bathroom stuff and brought it down last night.

Garrett's parents got in this morning and came right from the airport to see him. His mom cried, and they hugged me, but we didn't talk about too much. I think they were still processing it all.

Geo took them out to the ranch, where they'll stay, while here. Since Geo has been taking care of the ranch, Garrett's dad said he'd help, too. I'm sure he wants something to keep him busy because we are all just waiting for Garrett to wake up.

It's been three days, and the nurse and doctor keep saying he should wake up any time now. The nurse told me again when she stepped in to check on him.

"I'm really hating that phrase," I mumble.

Behind me, my dad chuckles, "Me too, sweetheart."

My phone dings, and it's Becca checking in. Keeping one hand in Garrett's, I answer her that there's no change, and we're still just waiting.

I finish texting her when there's a light knock on the door. I look up to find Carter Grant and his wife, Janie, at the door with a brown bag.

"Violet sent us with some food," Janie says, as she takes the bag from Carter.

"And to check and see how you're doing," Carter says.

"Still just waiting. I wish I had more news, but until he wakes up, we just don't know anything."

"Waiting is the worst. Would you like a bit of company?" Janie asks.

"That would be nice." I smile at her.

Janie is the pastor's daughter, and we never really ran in the same circles. Though, she has always been really nice to me and Garrett in the past.

"How about you take a walk with me? I could use some fresh air," my dad says to Carter.

Cater looks over hesitantly at Janie, who nods and gives him a big smile, before he agrees.

Janie sits with me, as I eat the food Violet packed. She tells me how she and Carter met. When she tells me about Carter throwing her over his shoulder and carrying her out of a bar, I laugh so hard, that tears form in my eyes.

Their love story is so cute. How he thought he was tricking her into marrying him, but she was in love with him, anyway. She goes on to tell me about some of the other ranchers in town that she suspects Violet had a hand in fixing up in one way or another.

By the time my dad and Carter get back, I feel like I've known Janie forever, and she promises to check back in on me in a few days. I hope to hang out with her because I need more local friends.

Once they leave, I look over at my dad.

"I've always liked Carter. I'm glad to see him settled down. You look a bit better, too. I think some girl time is what you needed," Dad says.

"I think so, too. For a little while, I was able to put aside the thoughts of being stuck in a hospital. It was nice. Plus, I really like Janie, and getting to know her better, took my mind off of things."

That's when a doctor steps in. I recognize him because he's been in here a few times.

"Any changes?" I ask him.

He gives me the same sad, pitiful smile that the nursing staff has mastered. So, I know without him even having to say a word, that nothing has changed. We are still waiting.

"No, we don't see any changes other than he's healing, and there's no infection from the cuts we stitched up. So, that's good news. It's not uncommon for the brain to shut down, after a traumatic event like this. The body has its own way of healing itself. I wish I could give you a time for when he will wake up, but if I'm honest, it could be in an hour or a few more days. We just don't know."

I want to yell and scream *what do you mean you don't know,'* but deep down, I know this isn't his fault, and he's trying the best he can. So, I paste on that fake smile I've used, since I walked into this building and nod. I wait for him to leave, and when he does, the wall I hide behind falls.

I look over at my dad, and he seems as frustrated as I am.

"I'm going to step out into the hallway for a minute," I say and walk out of the door.

The moment I'm in the hallway, I lean against the wall. It sucks seeing him like this, but it would be so much easier if he would just wake up, and let me know he's okay because the not knowing is the worst.

I can handle the cuts and scrapes, and I can deal with him having to be on bed rest, with managing medications, doctors' appointments, and even physical therapy. If only he would just wake up, I can handle everything else. I have so much to say, and not being able to say it, is killing me.

I shouldn't have waited. That night I should have gone after him, and not let him put this distance between us. Instead of spending the day with Becca, I should have been on the ranch, fighting for him. All the things I wish I could have changed, run through my mind over and over, as I sit here and wait. It's slowly driving me mad.

Taking a deep breath, a passing nurse asks if I'm okay. I give her the false smile and nod. I hate lying to them, but I'm sure they're used to it.

Then, I hear the most beautiful sound in the world.

My name.

Chapter 9

♥

Garrett

Fuck, my head hurts. Am I hungover? I don't remember drinking this much, since my twenty-first birthday, and even then, I don't think my head hurt this badly.

I try to open my eyes, and even though there isn't much light in the room, it still hurts to open them. Before I close my eyes again, I get enough of a glimpse around to see I'm in a hospital room.

Then, it all comes back to me. The drive, the cow, and the car accident. Shit, no wonder I hurt pretty much everywhere. I crack my eyes open again and find Kaylee's dad, sitting on the couch across the room, reading a book.

If he's here, she has to be, right?

"Kaylee," I call out, my voice scratchy and not sounding like my own.

Her dad's head jerks up and looks at me before he stands, but I don't see what happens next, because Kaylee's walking in the door, her eyes on me, and my world feels right. She's here.

She rushes to my side and takes my hand in hers with tears in her eyes.

"I'm so sorry." I croak out.

"No, I'm sorry." She has tears running down her face, as she hands me a cup of water.

My voice raspy, I say, "I knew as soon as I left Jasper that I was wrong, but I didn't know what to say. Then, I wanted to talk in person. After I figured out what to say, then I was coming after you."

"I came to the ranch to fight for you. I was the one that found you," she whispers.

"I love you, Kaylee," I say the words I have wanted to say, since the moment I left Jasper.

More tears fall, but her smile is blinding.

"I love you, too." She leans down to give me a gentle kiss.

The kiss doesn't last long, because a doctor and a nurse file into the room and start asking me all sorts of questions. If I know where I am, who I am, who the people in the room are, what day it is, and all that stuff to make sure I don't have any memory loss.

They conclude I'm fine, but want to run a few tests, before they send me home.

Once the doctor and nurse leave, I turn back to Kaylee. She hasn't let go of my hand the whole time they were here, and the nurse didn't seem surprised about it.

"You've been here the entire time?" I ask.

"She has and hasn't left your side. Your parents are here, Geo has been in and out, and Violet has sent people with food to check in as well." Her dad says.

"That sounds about right." I chuckle, just as my mom and dad walk into the room.

There's more hugs, more questions about how I'm feeling, and what the doctor said. Mom goes on to tell me about all the food she made to restock my freezer, and my dad talks about the ranch. Through it all, I can't take my eyes off Kaylee.

She's here, and she's mine.

·♥·♥·♥·♥·♥·

Last night, was the first night back in my own bed, and it felt wonderful. Being back in a space that's mine, being able to have Kaylee in my arms, and not being woken up every few hours, is wonderful.

The only downside is waking up alone this morning. It's slow going getting up and moving to the kitchen. My ribs hurt, and I have to make my movements slow and deliberate.

When I make it, I'm rewarded by the sight of my girl making coffee.

"Hey, I was going to bring you breakfast in bed," she pouts.

"I need to get out of bed."

"No, you need to rest."

"I will rest in the living room with the better TV."

She glares at me before she sighs.

"Fine. Your dad is spending the day down at the barn. I guess one of the cows is giving birth. Your mom went into Jasper to get some stuff for the house. Though, I wouldn't be surprised, if she redecorates it. She's been inspired by what Jordyn is doing. I have to run into work to check on things, and I have a meeting with my boss. Then, I'm grabbing some of my stuff too, so my dad is coming to sit with you," she says.

"I don't need a babysitter," I groan.

"You kind of do. You still need help getting to the bathroom, and you can't stand long enough to cook yet. But I know, if you get bored, you will get up and try to find something to do. So, Dad will come and make sure you aren't bored, feed you lunch, and basically make sure you follow doctor's orders until I get back."

"You are just as bad as my mom when I broke my leg in middle school."

"I can be worse if you don't do as you're told."

"Okay, okay." I raise my hands in surrender.

"I will sit and talk to your dad and watch TV until you get back. I promise."

"If you want to talk ranch stuff, your dad and Geo can come up to the house, but you are not to go to the barn today."

"I promise." I try to hide the smile on my face because I love her taking care of me.

Just as I finish my breakfast and make it to the couch, her dad shows up. She gives him the rundown of what I can and can't do, and then gives me a kiss and is out the door.

"So, are you going crazy not being able to do anything yet?" Her dad asks as he joins me in the living room.

"It was nice to be in my own bed, but yeah, it feels weird to be sitting around, when I know how much work there is to be done."

"If I know my daughter, she has it all under control," he chuckles.

"Speaking of your daughter." I decide to bite the bullet, instead of sitting on this all day and possibly missing my chance.

Mr. Mitchell has to know what's coming because he goes serious and sits up straight.

"I love her. I always have, even if I didn't want to admit it to myself. She's my best friend and the better half of me. We had an argument, before the accident, that I'm sure she's told you all about. But it made me realize what she means o me. I'd like your permission to ask her to marry me."

He stares at me, giving nothing away, before he speaks.

"I'm not sure. You do have a playboy reputation around town, you know. That's not quite the type of guy I pictured for my daughter."

My heart sinks. Geo told me many times that was going to come and bite me in the ass, and now he's right.

"I'm not sure how the reputation started. Maybe, I got it after I had gone out with three different girls in a month. I was too picky. It seemed I was looking for someone better than Kaylee. I was comparing them all to her, and when they didn't hold up, I dumped them. Though I didn't sleep around, I just dated a lot. I was an idiot, because there's no one better than Kaylee.

"No, there isn't," her dad agrees.

"She had big dreams to go off to school, and I didn't want to be the one to stop her, so I kept her in the friend zone. She did the same for me. But I won't lie, I did everything I could to make sure she didn't get serious with anyone."

"Oh, I know, and she was pretty pissed at you for it."

"I don't regret it, and I'd do it all over again if it meant I'd end up with her."

He doesn't say anything but looks me over like he's trying to get me to crack under pressure, but I'm not backing down. Not when it comes to this.

"I know about the pact you two made. She got drunk one night and was mad at you and let it slip. I always knew even before then that you two would end up together. When I saw the way you looked at one another, and how close you were, it was obvious. You'd have been blind not to see it. Garrett, I'd be honored to call you family, even though you already are."

Relief floods me, and a smile takes over. I have his blessing, and I know that will be important to her.

Her dad goes on, "I have her mother's ring set. It was her favorite, so I saved it for her. You stop by the house and have dinner with me one night, and I'll give it to you. Now, put on that new spy movie. I've been waiting to see it."

Just like that, I'm watching a movie with my future father-in-law, and I have a path for the life I want. There are just a few details to work out when Kaylee gets back.

It's only been a few hours, and I miss her like crazy. I can't wait to start planning the rest of our lives together.

·❤·❤·❤·❤·❤·

Kaylee

Driving into Whiskey Run, so many memories flood me. The days I was in school and would come home for the weekend. The plans Garrett would make for us.

He's done so much to make things work between us, and not just as friends. Now, it's my turn to take control and show him we can make this work.

It's been a long day, and I had so much to do in Jasper, that if it weren't for Becca and a little help from her bother, I might not have gotten it all done. She's so happy for me, and I'm beginning to think this was her plan all along because I expected her to be more upset about me ditching Jason like I did.

After a quick stop at my dad's house, I pull into the ranch, and Geo meets me at my car.

"He didn't come out to the barn. When I checked on him earlier, he had fallen asleep after lunch, while watching TV with your dad."

"Good, the pain medicine they have him on probably knocked him out."

Then, I grab the bag I packed and take it in the house with me. I find Garrett and my dad still in the living room both watching TV.

"Hey, sweetheart. He did good and didn't overdo it. Ate lunch, took his meds, and even took a nap." My dad says, standing and kissing me on the cheek. "Now, I'm going home."

"You don't want to stay for dinner?" I ask.

"No, I have a buddy coming over who's in town for a few days. Call me if you need anything."

"I will, Dad." Then, I hug him and join Garrett on the couch. Leaning in, I give him a kiss.

"I missed you," he says.

"I missed you, too. Now, what do you want for dinner?" I ask and start to stand, but he takes my hand in his.

When I turn back to him, I know that serious face. He has something he wants to talk about, and he doesn't want to wait.

"I really love you being here," he says.

"I like being here, too. And I'm missing this place more than I should when I'm in Jasper."

"How is this going to work? Your work and apartment are in Jasper, and I'm here. As friends, we've made it work, but we are more now and..."

I decide to cut him off before his brain goes down a dangerous path.

"That's why I was in Jasper today." I stop him, and he doesn't even hide the shock that crosses his face.

"What?" He asks.

"Sitting in the hospital waiting for you to wake up, I had a lot of time to think. I realized I wasn't really happy in Jasper anymore, and it was time to make some changes. So, I had a meeting with my boss, and as of today, I'm officially able to work from home. I only have to go into Jasper a few times a month for meetings. Becca and her brother helped me box up my apartment."

He shifts to look at me better. "What?" He asks again in shock, so I keep speaking.

"Before I came over here, I dropped a bunch of stuff off at my dad's, and Becca and her brother are taking the furniture they want and bringing me the rest of my boxes next weekend. They'll have dinner here to officially meet you. I gave my landlord my thirty-day notice. I'm moving back to Whiskey Run, and back to my dad's."

"No, you aren't." He says in his firm I'm not messing around voice, and my heart sinks.

I'm moving too fast, and I should have talked to him first. Of course, this is moving too fast for the Whiskey Run playboy. Either way, this is what I want. I want more time with my dad, and I want out of the city, so I'm doing this.

"Yes, I am," I say. "I'm doing this for me. If you still only want to see me on weekends, then so be it, but I want to be closer to my dad."

He's shaking his head and smiling. Maybe, the pain meds have made him lose his mind.

"What I mean is you aren't moving in with your dad. I want you to move in here with me."

"You do?" I ask startled.

"Of course, I do. I want to see you every day. And to know you are here just a few feet away, and that I can stop in for a kiss any time I want," he smirks.

"I have a feeling you'll be stopping in for more than a kiss."

He shrugs, but then takes my hand in his again and pulls me towards him and onto his lap. I settle there as gingerly as I can, but he still cringes from the movement.

"Once I was feeling better, I was planning this whole big thing. It was going to be over the top and magical, maybe even under the stars, but I don't think I can wait that long. I want to marry you, baby girl, and I don't want to wait on our pact to do it. I want to marry you now, run the ranch with you, and have kids with you now. Don't make me wait. Will you marry me?"

Is he kidding? I want nothing more, but I really thought we were moving too fast. I should have known this is my Garrett, and we have always been on the same wavelength, even when we were mad at each other.

"Of course, I'll marry you." I throw my arms around his neck and hug him tight.

He lets out a low groan, and I pull back. "I'm sorry."

"I'm not." He leans in and kisses me softly. "I have a ring, but it's not here yet. But then again, I hadn't planned to ask you tonight."

"I don't even need a ring. I just need you."

It's then his parents walk in the door, and the house comes to life. The life I pictured, but never thought would be mine, is right here at my fingertips.

Certainly, never thought I'd get it this way.

Epilogue

♥

Kaylee

6 years later

There's nothing like being woken up by being ninja kicked in the bladder by your unborn child, who is playing with their father.

Garrett loves playing with our little one now that she's more responsive to him. She'll stick out her foot against the side of my stomach, and he'll tickle it, and she will jerk it away, hitting whatever organ is in her way.

This is what I woke up to this morning. Garrett is leaning over my large stomach with a huge smile on his face, playing with our little girl and talking to her about his plans for the ranch today. It's not like she has any clue what moving the cows to the north pasture really means.

"Now you've done it. You have gone and woken up your momma. I told you she needed her sleep today." He says, before kissing my belly, and then turning his eyes to me.

"Good morning, my beautiful wife." He greets me like he does every morning. I joke with him for a bit, but he says it's to remind me that I'm his. "Good morning, my husband." I stretch a bit and give him a kiss, before heading to the bathroom, as I get ninja kicked again.

This cabin he rented for the weekend may be out of the way and near the mountains, but it has a bathroom to rival a luxury hotel. Heck, the toilet seat has a warmer, which is pretty nice first thing in the morning.

When I walk back out to the bedroom, there's a large gift in the center of the bed, but Garrett is nowhere to be found. I open the box, and inside, I find the bedding I wanted for our little girl.

We had been arguing for a week over which bedding, because he didn't want pink, but I did. I just laugh, because if I know my husband, this was planned from the start, and he was always going to give in.

I run my hand over the soft blanket, before heading to the rest of the cabin in search of Garrett, where I find him in the kitchen making breakfast. I walk up behind him and hug him as close as my belly will allow anyway, kissing his shoulder.

He turns and wraps one around mine and smiles. "Go sit down. I'll bring you some orange juice."

I do as he asks and stare out of the window at the beautiful mountain views. I have always loved The Smoky Mountains, and this was the perfect spot for a babymoon, as his parents are calling it. They are at home with our son and loving having all his attention to themselves right now.

After we got married, it wasn't long, before I was more interested in the ranch than my job. After talking it over with not only Garrett, but Geo, Becca, and my dad, and

Violet had an opinion too, I finally put in my notice, left my job, and became a full-time ranch wife.

Working alongside Garrett on the ranch has been everything we always dreamed it would be, and our food costs went down because I was able to menu plan and head into Jasper to shop sales and bulk buy.

The first month, when I spent half of what the guys had been, they thought we'd run out of food, but I was able to get more by stopping at the local grocery store every few days.

Thinking back on Geo's shock, still makes me laugh.

"What's so funny over there?" Garrett asks.

I guess I was laughing at the memory.

"Nothing much. Just thinking about, when I first moved into the ranch."

"I have a confession to make." He sits down with me and places my plate in front of me.

"Oh, yeah?"

"This isn't just a babymoon, as my mom put it."

I stop and think. It's not either of our birthdays, and it's not our anniversary, so I'm not sure what this weekend is.

"What is it?"

"This is the weekend I had planned to propose to you per the pact we made."

Holy shit. That is this year, isn't it? I had completely forgotten about it.

"I'm glad we didn't wait." I smile at him.

"Me too. Being married to you has been the best thing to ever happen to me. Our kids have made me happier than I ever thought possible, and you make me happier than I ever dreamed. This life we have is what I always pictured.

I just didn't think we'd be able to start it so soon." He pulls me onto his lap.

Then, he rests his hand on my belly, like he always does, when I'm in reach. Like he's ready to protect anyone or anything that tries to get near. When his mom and dad come up to touch my belly, it also irritates him. He doesn't like anyone touching me, and I love how protective he is.

He was protective of our son, and he loves showing him how to do new things on the ranch, but I have a feeling, when our little girl is born, he will be extra protective of her and will be training our son to do the same thing.

Heck, if I'm being honest, I'm sure Geo and all the ranch hands will be extra protective. Garrett gets that from his dad. I've seen how his dad is with his mom, and as soon as they heard we were having a girl, they made plans to move back to Whiskey Run.

They were just going to buy a small place in town, but Garrett insisted they live on the ranch. So, they picked a small plot of land far enough from the main house for us both to have some privacy and then built a cabin for themselves. They moved in last week, and our son, Alex, is staying with them this weekend.

My dad has officially retired, and we even offered to build him a cabin on the other side of the ranch from Garrett's parents, but he wants to stay in town. He's become a bit of a social butterfly. He goes to the library a few times a week, has dinner at the diner to keep up on local gossip, meets up with friends several times a week, and even started volunteering. I think he has a better social life now than I ever did.

The second Garrett removes his hands from my belly so that he can feed me, our little girl kicks, and she kicks hard.

"I guess she isn't too happy to not have your attention," I grunt, as she kicks again.

The moment he places his hand back on my belly, she settles down.

"She's already a daddy's little girl," I joke.

"I wouldn't have it any other way." He says, kissing me.

My life may not have gone according to plan, but I think it turned out so much better.

My cowboy is committed to me and our family, and that's all I ever wanted.

·♥·♥·♥·♥·♥·

Want more Whiskey Run Cowboy Lover Curves?
Whiskey Run is home to the sexiest and most possessive cowboys you'll ever find. They work hard and play even harder. They might be gruff and bossy, but all it will take is the right curvy woman to bring them to their knees. Welcome to Whiskey Run... where the cowboys know how to ride.
<u>Check out the series!</u>
Rescuer Cowboy by Mia Brody
Obsessed Cowboy by Hope Ford
Virgin Cowboy by Kat Baxter
Tempted Cowboy by Frankie Love
Committed Cowboy by Kaci Rose

·♥·♥·♥·♥·♥·

If you want even more cowboys make sure to check out my Rock Springs Texas series starting with **<u>The Cowboy</u>**

<u>**and His Runaway.**</u>

You can get a **free Rock Springs Novella** by joining my Newsletter as well.

<u>**https://www.kacirose.com/free-books/**</u>

Connect with Kaci Rose

♥

Website
Facebook
Kaci Rose Reader's Facebook Group
TikTok
Instagram
Twitter
Goodreads
Book Bub
Join Kaci Rose's VIP List (Newsletter)

<u>The Cowboy and His Mistletoe Kiss</u> – Lilly and Mike
<u>The Cowboy and His Valentine</u> – Maggie and Nick
<u>The Cowboy and His Vegas Wedding</u> – Royce and Anna
<u>The Cowboy and His Angel</u> – Abby and Greg
<u>The Cowboy and His Christmas Rockstar</u> – Savannah and Ford
<u>The Cowboy and His Billionaire</u> – Brice and Kayla

Mountain Men of Whiskey River
<u>Take Me To The River</u> – Axel and Emelie
<u>Take Me To The Cabin</u> – Pheonix and Jenna
<u>Take Me To The Lake</u> – Cash and Hope
<u>Take Me To The Mountain</u> – Bennett and Willow

Standalone Books
<u>Stay With Me Now</u> – David and Ivy
<u>Texting Titan</u> - Denver and Avery
<u>Accidental Sugar Daddy</u> – Owen and Ellie
<u>She's Still The One</u> – Dallas and Austin
<u>Midnight Rose</u>
<u>Committed Cowboy</u> – Whiskey Run Cowboys

I love to hear from my readers! Please **head over to Amazon and leave a review** of what you thought of this book!